THRU THE FIRE

VINCENT WARE

Published by Julia House Publishing
P.O. Box 2811, Inglewood, Ca. 90305

Printed in the U. S. A.

CONTENTS

FOREWARD

I have never written anything like a foreward and I never really cared about doing so. For if there is any sense to writing one, it might very well be in the advantage it seems to have over other texts in the very choice it leaves to the reader to ignore it altogether. Such an alternative becomes some kind of incentive to get to the object the foreward proposes to introduce, namely, the actual book that one has decided to read. Yet, there are some people who do like them. They share something in common with those who enjoy more a main course after they have had some appetizer. It is chiefly to them that these lines are intended.

"Thru The Fire" is by no means an arbitrary title, nor does it proceed from the will to fulfill the intention to provide a book of poetry with a wrapping bearing the label of some poetic effect, though it may as well do so in spite of the author's purpose. Had it not been for Vincent Ware's own experience of the crossing of those burning rivers that await, sometimes the human condition, such a title, which after all does not seek to be exclusive, could have concerned an entirely different type of book.

The fire which the author speaks of is nurtured at the never dying flames rising from his will to love. For in love, Vincent sees the threshold of all quest, and in love, too does he see the medium through which to interrogate the silence of man's destiny. Hence, the image of woman is undoubtedly the first and last figure in which the quest of love itself is being clothed, the supreme garment of a man's desire. And if such a desiring man were to reach the object of his passion beyond its image, such a man is, in the author's understanding, free from the fears that only love in a veiled appearance may inspire. Such a man now possesses the key which was forged in that same fire that threatened to consume him, together with his passion and his quest. With this key he will surely open the doors of the self, the only place where love is to be found in its permanence.

Each of the four books constituting "Thru The Fire" is one of the steps toward this unveiling process and each book reveals a specific poetry, a unique rendition.

In the poetry of Vincent Ware, it seems that the poet relies more in the rhythm pertaining to the scenes he depicts than in their actual picturing. Not that his wording is not colorful. Nor that it is not speaking to the senses. Only, the rhythm from which this author modulates through as many given scenes, is here to make the respiration of his own words more lively. However, this seems less perceptible to consciousness, just as we do not take notice of when we inhale and exhale in breathing naturally. For this reason

"White Rains," as it opens the first book of the tetralogy reads as the beginning of a story rather than that of a poem, regardless of its definite poetic form. Also, its agitated tempo unfolds a sequence of dramatic events which becomes clear mostly by means of a tonal articulation.

In both "Window Pain" and "Redemptive Journeys," the narration does not part from its dramatic tone. It is permeated by such changing intensities that one comes to wonder whether the author casts, now and then, an eye on his own odyssey, or whether these changes are--in the story he actually confesses--those same changes which were imposed on his perception at the time he underwent the related events. Thus, by the time we are making the transition to the final book, "Resolutions," we are definitely expecting an answer to these ambiguities, for we have gone too far already, along with the narrator's emotions, not to know what he will decide to do with them. This may also be due to Vincent Ware's peculiar way of telling a story. For he is, as a story teller, less concerned by the very poetic essence of the facts of life than he is in the possibility of communicating to us the life that lies under its facts. Which is precisely what the essence of poetry is about.

Olivier Reghay

And we may well heave a sigh of relief at the thought that it is nevertheless vouchsafed to a few to salvage without effort from the whirlpool of their own feelings the deepest truths, towards which the rest of us have to find our way through tormenting uncertainty and with restless groping.

Sigmund Freud

WHITE RAINS

BOOK I

1969 - 1982

Days Turn Dark
Black Like The Night
Worlds Turn Cold
Rains Turn White

TABLE OF CONTENTS

There's a time of year
I feel you
so very close to me.
This is when I think about you
and dream about you most of all.

No leaves are left for raking.
I loved to breathe their autumn burning.

The trees all standing naked
have let their colors pall.

No ice cream bells are ringing.
I hear no songs of song birds singing.
I saw them soaring thru grey skies
winging their way toward the warmth
toward their southern call.

My Darling,
I miss you in the Spring.
I know the loneliness Summer brings.
But I dread to see the flowers
begin their drying
and the leaves
turn golden red toward their dying.
For me this means the passing
of yet another Fall.

Next comes old cold Winter.
This is when I want you so badly.

This is when I dream about you most of all.

Winter,
with early sunsets
turned off the sun, turned off the lights.
Winter,
with artic mornings, evening darkness
and glistening sights.
Winter,
with rain drops blowing sideways
wet
and cold
and white.

Each November I remember
your fires, how you warmed me,
your desires, how you burned me.
Your lips so soft would passionately kiss me.
Your body, supple, so very close to me.
You would embrace me, squeeze me
and hug me so very tight.

I glowed and smoldered in the daytime
from the love that you had given.
I shivered with ecstasy
thru long, long winter nights.

Winter,
the season when you left me.
Death,
the reason, can never be quite right.

Winter,
and I look across the vast stillness
of the freshly fallen snow.
The memories of my loves for you
that are frozen deep, deep within my soul
compels me to follow those first footprints
although I know I hesitate to go
around that same corner along that icy road.

There was where I found you
all alone that wintry night.

And the rain that settled on you gently
was wet
and cold,
and white.

Although
I've never cast mine eyes upon you.
I've never seen your lovely face.

Also,
I have not known the fires
from the heats of your embrace.

Yet,
my every-day-dreams upset me
my nights know not their place.

And,
it seems already I've been here
twice before I've watched this race.

Still,
I'm breathlessly awaiting you
with apprehension but just a trace.

If,
sometimes my thoughts out-weigh me
they're made through impatient's haste.

But,
I cannot resist these cravings
or these urges of you to taste.

Because,
I know not how long we'll be here
sweet times we must not waste.

What could it be
that spins her from me?
What is it that makes her unable to see?

Why can't she realize
that my feelings lie
within Lust of the tears
that fall from my eyes?

Oh why can't my stares
force impending love's wetness
within her to rise?
Why can't I mouthe into being
her suppressed Lustful sighs?

Why won't my whispers force her to turn
and allow the moist darkness
of her bodies to burn?

Does she know my caresses
will allow her to scream?
Does she know that my kisses
are what ecstasy means?

Perhaps she doesn't know
that for her wetness to draw me within
would mean
I could tenderly suck her beginning
a lifetime beyond its end.

Or maybe she's confused
and slightly afraid
of Lust she possesses
and why she was made.

Then again maybe she believes
that although she comes with Lust
Lust comes with control,
and this is what allows her
to contain her Lustful Soul.

Oh why can't she know?
She just can't remember
of the gentle beauty of giving in
and the meaning of surrender?

She would throb with the wonders
and understand how Lust is real.
She would wail out jagged moans of thunder
and spasm from the lightning
I would cause her to feel.

She would plead and beg for me not to heed
her cries and sighs
that are sounding like stop.
She would push me and pull me
throughout her need
and urge on then surge on over the top.

She would wail out her soul
just could not take it
the mountain was rising
she just couldn't make it.

Then screaming a sigh
as if she would die
her soul would explode
and shower the sky.

And then finally knowing
love's peaks are alive
she'll understand this Love's growings
and burning Lust she'll realize.

And in each other's arms
with the red suns in our eyes
she'll love this new freedom
of rising mountains that
SWALLOW
OUR
SKIES

Left?
Nothing but remembrances
and visions
of a once ago time.

Thoughts?
I did not know you.
I could not touch you,
being
you were only in my mind.

Words?
There,
but suppressed unspoken.
Sounds
I just could not find.

Feeling?
Why can't I have you?
Give me a moment
a reason, a rhyme.

Going?
My head down thinking,
off she stepped
into the line.

Going?
I felt I saw Her
and I followed
as if I were Blind.

Going.
Just like the dawning
that's withdrawing the darkness
from an endless night.
She was fading,
and then she vanished
like dreams it seems do
in daylight.

Goodbye.
Thanks for the brief
chance meeting
much too short and
much too fast
by course that's
much too fleeting.

To be left alone will never be right.
Goodbye.
Yet even in leaving
I'll forever remember your smiling eyes
and from mine eyes
shall you never leave my sight.

I talked amongst the mid-day moons
and wondered once again how soon
the growing feelings within my heart
would entice me to my rainbow's start.

I laid upon the furthest star
and wonderd was it very far
through the coldness to your wholeness
to the Love-land where you are.

I walked the water's curving bends
and slept upon their beds and then,
moaned aloud for my rainbow's end.

I warmed myself on the mid-night suns
bewildered as whether or not to run away, away.

To stay would daze me once again.
The hazy way would blindly begin.
My teardrop colors would run down then
and my arc would feel of if and when.

So on I run, on I fly
past your Moonsuns to your love land sky.
And on I wail, on I cry
and deeply sigh from deep within
doubting my realness
will one day send
to you Love,
my Love
at our Rainbow's

END.

I feel time's sands
run between my hands
and fear Love Land
may not understand
another longing man.

Wondering thus,
I feel Miss Midnight Dream
no matter how soon it seems,
my touch to your touch
is still a yesterday's must.

I recognize that size,
and I've run the length
and strong is the strength
of my rushing desire.

So why must you embrace Mrs. Concerned
when Moment's love should be learned,
to churn,
and burn,
and progress the depths and turns
of your life.

Love helps,
even if it's only felt
from midnight to mourn.

Running Love does exist
through the caress
and through the Gentle kiss.

Love is love
when it's felt of.

And know this.
It shoves deep from the depths
and highs far above.

Despised or Realized Miss Midnight Dream
it exists,
and Hesitant time idolizes fading Resist.

So together let us spin
Love's twenty-four hour wheels.
And together sensitive one
some grains of sand we'll steal.
And our relation
born of one moment's Love sensation
will last beyond the duration
of the twinkling sands
OF
LOVE'S
CREATION.

There was Ethel
and Gretal and Rita,
and one whose name I will never find out.

For we had drank and laughed together.
In the end then
they had walked out.

If only
they would have liked me and stayed,
eventually,
they would have found out.

They could have learned
of the wants inside me,
and the thoughts
that I think I'm about.
Why most times
are our feelings hidden
unspoken, ergo
Forbidden,
and therefore
left inside not out.

Remember.
Inside never out
are deep seeded problems.
Inside they'll reside.
For inside one cannot solve them.

Yet, in my mind
the taste of you
will help resolve them.
A drink of your warmth
with its wetness
is a solvent.

Fires of Desire
can never be put out.
In order for them to be
they must be set free
somehow they must be let out.

A man alone,
if he's alone then he's without.
Too long alone,
Too much inside.
It's so wrong
to be long without.

You hesitate
and I procrastinate
we smile yet we both still doubt.
You get up and leave
I wander to the next one
for I'm just a spigot
without a spout.

And my feelings buried deep inside
are inside.
And inside is inside
not out.

You made me glance upon the plains
I saw the wind swept mountains
you demanded I accept the sane
I claim I cannot count them
For they are like a somber star
so close and yet a distant far.

And you whose name is Properly
yes you who represent the free,
you cause a haze I sway and swoon
I gaze upon the dark half moon
high noon and yet your time's too soon.

Why must your way cause misery
and bring my fears down onto me?
Why can't your lamps by which you see
take me, shake me, guide me free?

Why? Because your light glares low
and leads me where I dare not go.
Your lands are filled with I don't know
and maybe yes perhaps it's so.
And I am made of hopes and dreams
and that's what's there or so it seems
and I revel in sweet abandon
no levels, just the streets of Random.

And that my Love is no Direction?
No choice? Of course there's no selection.
But Love life's paths we must elect one
and make our World this time's Exception.

My Life,
I know that issued words of mine
cannot coax nor smoke the apprehensiveness
from your mind,
and thustly insure that all is indeed well.
Yet it's true that for us
rigid worlds and standing stagnant time
is a hoax and a mirage
for Love's relentlessness
is a knotted rope and steel taut line.

As though certain your last breath,
you swell your lungs and breathe.
This so, your breast throbs and heaves
doubt and uncertainty
for you will not leave.
Lonely, longing lasting eternities
have not allowed you, yourself to relieve.

Alone and along the paths and mazes
we stagger stumble
soothe our bruises
and remove the grainy pebbles
from our faces hands and knees.
And deep within surrenderings rumble
and sleep, it ends
as we toss and tumble
and fall,
we fall torn asunder and humble
cast in to wander,
left out to wonder.

Where lies the powers the strengths?
How much longer the hours
how much stronger the jaunted lengths?
What consists of salvation?
What exists? What formation?

You and I are the formula.
You and I are the creation.
With my loves for you
and all yours for me,
we will skim the Tidal Waves
of problem times.
Never again we won't.
Forever again we'll be.
Together my love
we will waltz the troubled seas.

Thus if we believe,
we can,
we must conceive.
There's no dreaming there is meaning
in these words to you I tell.
Faith,
for in this race
all is good,
when all ends well.

It's as though it's an entwining
and seeping mist,
or perchance it's a soft enchanting kiss.
This is the path that created the miss
and thrusted me within a fading bliss.

This love's fling this sweet love train
is a Devastating thing.
It's cruel and unjust
and it's born from deep pain.

And now never so much have I wanted to die.
How clever the touch
of an unrequited cry.

Not once before has my candle flamed so low.
I've felt it, I have felt it
and I've hardened after I've melted
yet finally I could feel it was so.

A sourful Love is a Powerful Love.
I have suffered I have suffered
until at last I now know.

There is no love there is no love
there's no such thing as Love.

It's a self-effacing scheme
a tragic and unmagic dream
and it seems
it's one that we all are singing of.

I panic and I'm frantic
this can't be as it should.
It's not good, it's no good
it just can't be any good.

I'm unhappy and I hurt and it burns
to my very core.
It's unlike anything else
that I have ever experienced before.

Yet it's Love elusive Love
that has wrenched
this traumatic change.
I've seen it squandered
and it's made me ponder
and wonder how it can be so strange.

Now I'm weak from the unremitting pressure
I can no longer withstand the strain.

Murder me Sweet Love.
Release the lethal ache
and allow me to lie down.

My salvation is the cold sensation
I will re-live
when I'm buried in the ground.

What loves the Love?
What does this Love feel of?

The Falseness of Eternal Lives
where Death is not believed,
or conceived of?

The untruth of Another
possessing the being that is among
yet above all others?

The blindness of Deceit
wraps forth an embrace with which
all the other Love Worlds, and the stars meet.
As long as the lengths of this truth:
There is a Dying that falls
sputtering and spinning
within the dimming,
from one love's ending
through another love's beginning.
There to once again shove
that once again Love.
That is how strong that is the strength
that consists within the pain
that there does live false songs.

This truth makes this Love wrong.

This Love makes this resistance
and this terrifying existence.

Yes! There Lies the loves of Love.
There is what Love loves.
Then what feels the Heart
when love has passed the start
making an ending
a necessary beginning?

It feels a longing to die,
that's what the Heart feels.

What sigh the Tears
when the Liquids of burning love
are stirred enough by fears
to rise and then appear?

A longing to die
that's what the Tears cry.

And now where goes the love
that Love could not want
that was made a shame of?

It cups the warmth of Hurt
and sucks the wishful body of Longing.
It steals away to glance away
in hopes of a meeting again.

Only then can the pain of Falseness emerge.
Only then can the pain of love submerge.
Only then can Love
love on.

I stretched my gaze onto the sky

I spied a moonlit night.
I recognized the darkness
and I marveled at the light.

When I cried and started moaning
then I knew what was not right
for we had parted in the morning,
you had flown to take your flight.

As I stood there dying I trembled
I could not suppress the fright
while descending all around me
were flakes of lonely white.

Now I'm alone and I am blinded
please return to me my sight.
You must bridge this gap of distances
and somehow transcend the heights.

For just the presence of your being
and it matters not how slight
will stoke red coals of Love
and make my moon burn bright.

And,
now how are you
sweet warm life that I touch?

Are you even now living such?

Are you life living
as coldly as the ritually performed killing
of the hollow red sphere that deathly sleep
meets
in the east?

Or are you life doing
as blindly as that streaking world pursuing
home
roams?
Shockingly scattering its desire
until at last the fire
fades
away?

Or are you life dying as moaningly
as that painful fear that is holding me
within you
slips,
to fall
and dreamingly
floats me
upon a wavy hazy sea
that forces me
to wail?

Yes I wail the wail that deafly fails
to loosen the feeling that I long to prevail.

Within each new reflection,
and at each love loving section,
I battered an erection
of you jagged life.

And at my heart's every junctures,
beyond life
a step past death
with a linger at the WINDOW SILL OF HELL,
you forever managed to deeply puncture,
for I forever managed to bleed well.

For I wonder for you
and I forget the number of you
so that even now as I dream
I still kiss the square lava
that mysteriously steams
from the last endless tunnel I flew
thru
of you
dear life.

You forever hanging tear
you,
you that holds and chokes
my only feeling fear
did remain near.

Until.
I killed one world
and the next world then
became the same time when
I faded from the sky
but no longer able to bleed
hugged the earth and refused to die.

Yes!
Yes you did rise with cries.

Until.
I once eastwardly plunged my now frozen me
into a living scalding earthly sea
but rose with my soul
breathed a scent that was sent
by an invisible cloud that was meant
for all times to be spent

floating free

floating free.

Being me,

being me.

With yet my true life to live still,
I turned with a laugh
from your hell's window sill.

I passed among your one last vast field
and not once did I reach
not once did I feel
that I should cry to your sky,
PLEASE GOODNESS
don't let me die.

For you were no longer real.

Remain for-real forever
I remember I will.

Me,
will be
that smoothly floating honey brown
honey sea
that flows twenty two and four lifetimes
beyond your end of eternity.

All by just being me.

FLOATING
  FLOWING
    CURVLY TURNING
      BLACKLY BURNING

        FREE.

I'm so alone and lonely
and, OH, it hurts me so.
It hurts invisible Love.
Why by you must I be teased?
Lost Love, I cannot force myself to believe
that you must hurt before you can please.

I'm so alone and lonely.
And so unfound Love,
I long and mourn for you.
For you!
For you Love and you only.
No longer can I bear this.
No longer can I consist,
of bleeding, of crying,
and needing and sighing.
Each wrenching sigh
that is snatched from me,
weakens me.
I know this.
I feel this.
For I know the strength of Caged Desire.

> *Its wants exist within*
> *the creation of life.*
> *I was born from, within, without,*
> *throughout,and now out.*
> *Desire IS LIFE.*
> *and now She's turned and sank her fangs*
> *into Frustration,*
> *and made Him Her Wife.*

I'm so alone and lonely.
and Love, night Love, where are you?
You see that my mind and my heart
are burning with fever.
Yet you stand and stare beside my death-bed.
Only once
have you clasped together your hands,
and even then you continued to stand.
And only once have you lowered your eyes
but continued to stare.
so only once
have I felt that you really could care.

Now only sometimes do I dream.
And I know what these dreams mean.

You have crawled upon me
and breathed into me,
and loved with me.
Then you lay beside me and touch me
until I can embrace sleep no longer.

I rise,and you rise, and you are gone.
And then hidden Love, once again I am alone
and I know not of your return.

I lay then, to touch then,
the once again pain and fears that are real
and shiver in the dampness
from the tears I spill.

I cannot bear on much longer.
My steps are now so unsure I simply
lie in my wetness.
My Life's Desire has for the last time
stumbled and fell.
HELP ME!
Come turn me over, away from this spell.
Help make me able to plead for you,
and beg for you and long for you.
Come turn me over so that I can see you
if you float by.
PLEASE!
I must be able to look up.

> *Then when the darkness releases my moon*
> *and returns it to your suns in your sky*
> *the shadows will ease from my face,*
> *and warmth will smother me,*
> *and the tears*
> *will become steam in my eyes.*

It hurts so awfully bad.
And although I knew you kneeled beside me
when I breathed out your scent,
and although
I felt you caress the back of my heart
and the back of my mind,
I knew My love you would never find.

I even felt the tears
cascading from your eyes,
and ever so slightly, for just a beat,
your memory returned to me.
Then I lost you and then I knew,
there was no time left
for anything you could do.

You did return for me,
but you could never now turn me.
So She had at last
released her fangs from Frustration,
and
  set
    me
      FREE.

Too painful to think. Too wanted to wait.
Too needed to allow to escape.

Wanting to feel. Wanting.

Terrified to leave. Begging to please

Feeling this,
I want you
TO
COME
TRUE

Rise
And
Fly
Away
Sweet bitter dream that I see

Lower
Myself

And please, please release me,
for you're taking me
too close to believability.
All I want to be,
is Lonely

Forever alone.

How does it feel to be Dreams?
For how many have you been a dream?

I stepped into a black void
and I could not see.
I blackly reached and grabbed only to touch,
feel and examine.
I first touched black eyes, eyes that could not
see
me.
My embrace created sight.

I next caressed the black heart.
My total feelings were felt.
I opened the black mind,
and poured me forth.

Lastly, I uncovered
the eighteen and four witch doctors
of silk that I had submerged into my soul.

We cried together
as we formed the impossible mould.
I cried.

The tears were meaning as they were streaming
streaming
streaming.
That, that which I wanted most
would send me away
because all I was doing was dreaming,
dreaming
dreaming

Of You. Womanly Dreams.
How does it feel to be Dreams?
Are you really more day or night?
Are you more than Insanities?
Are you really less than Pain?
Are Illusions really your sisters?
Is Hope really your mother
or are you simply another
orphan like me,
lonely?

Why Dreams
does the light of the white day
brush you away?
Stay!
Stay!

So Dreams, that most feeling part of you
had to most naturally step into our creation.
You and I traveled opposite each other
for so long.

Then once you came.
And I came.
I marveled!
You were actually the Dream.
You were actually the same that we all thought
ought to have been from the first
the only to remain untouched!

Rise
And
Fly
Away
Sweet bitter dream that I see.

I closed my eyes lowered my head
and moaned no,
no,
No.

The blackness
made you unable to recognize me,
your creator.
Yours.

And you possessed so much, so many.
My dreaming Walk, and talk and smile.
My dreaming Soul.

You smothered my face to your body
and I was unable to speak.
And had I been able,
would have still remained unable.

How can I not again touch and caress?
I want to hold you just once again.
With anticipation caused by satisfaction
would I then await the end.

Perhaps the lonely hot fire
will burn away
the rubble of forgetfulness.

I want you Dreams!
You are mine!
I want you!
It was you!
No one else!

It was you that I made!
Don't fade.

My breath comes short
and I wonder will I live on.
Time and time again
I have been made to understand
that I held not my real Dreams
but only a Nightmare.

But you
I will never leave to wander alone again.
You wander in a search
for the meaning of what your eyes see,
your heart feels,
and your mind understands.

Only I can teach you.
Only I can make you see
what your Dreams should be.
And Only the warmth of you
can make my Dreams come true.

So if you must go then,
fly away
sweet bitter dream that I see.
The sooner
the easier it will be for me.

Stay much longer,
and I won't be able to say
that you were just another
that was not supposed to stay.
Lover.

I've loved you for such a very long time.
I grow weary. I'm tired.
I want to stop. Stop me!
Please stop me,
and tell me,
how does it feel to be Dreams?
Do you feel for the ones you leave?
Do you feel me?
No?
Then there's only one Lonely thing
for you to do.

Either,
Fly away
Sweet bitter dream I see
or come.
Come with me
            and
                Come
                    TRUE.

The day after yesterday
I walked out upon the end of a dock that
ran to the end of itself. I just stood
there and gazed out among the metal.
Suddenly it became dark.
I closed my eyes to miss the black sunrise.
I could only stand there unwilling to move.
I felt so strange.
I had not felt that way for such a long time.
I had almost forgotten what it was like
to die.
I had almost forgotten what happened.
So I sat down with a handful of rain
and began to remember that
WHEN
I
DIE

I'll stop the world.
I'll grab that great spinning top
until it slows then stops.
and eternal rotation
will become hovering
suspended animation.

WHEN
I
DIE
(what will it look like?)
(will I recognize it?)

After one last taste
of the Nectar of the Universe,
after one last stare
at the Falling Water's rainbow,
after one last stop at the world I love,
I'll take myself, reach behind the sun
for Night's black sand
and sprinkle
the stars, the moon and the sun
out

WHEN
I
DIE
(what will it look like?)
(will I feel it?)

I'll float down.
Then I'll float upon
the repeating Blue Tides.
My new cold Being will wash to Shore.
I'll hold each one there.
Their anger will grow to Waves.
But I'll stretch them thin
and they will never return.
Never more will there be a Shore.

WHEN
I
DIE
(where will it come from?)

The hot running red tears of the Mountains
will melt them away.

The gliding birds
will stop,
to join the procession
and walk,
along side the Honey Bees and Flowers
that will talk, and sigh,
goodbye, goodbye

WHEN
I
DIE
(I wonder will I cry?)

And You! Then You!

You'll be stepping along
with your invisible face
and checkerboard heart
unaware that you're moving,
yet not moving from a standing still start.

I'll ease my shadow
over the remembrances of your mind.
And only so long
as you can staley inhale
will you live on

WHEN
I
DIE
(will love be holding my hand?)

You'll breathlessly scream for nothing.
You'll panic
with the one way wind.
Turn for me. Grope for me. Reach me.
And I'll suck away your last lives.
Take your breath which is my breath.
Then blow your eyes
shut.

WHEN
I
DIE
(when will Remember forget me?)

Gone will be the GOOD
hiding in the sky
Too soon. Too young. Too close.
Only two will not exist.
Hiding will not consist
of last moment whispered lies
toward the empty throne,
and disappearing skies.
There will be no list
of trails turning out.
There will be no out.
No need to ask why. You'll go when I go.
You'll go
WHEN
I
DIE
(I wonder will my bridge be high?)

Just relax and wait for the next time
you'll wastefully struggle
inside my next Black bubble.
Mine will be preparing to lay,
for only I could breathe Stay.
You'll dare not to, and I'll care not to

WHEN
I
DIE
(will my heart understand?)

I accept I'll step
to the rail of the bridge
and lean against it. Just to feel it.
I think I'll look down into It.
And I think I'll think a while.
Then I'll frown with resignation.
Then I'll smile a smile of confusion
as I pull forth that whispered voice
that sometimes romps with Illusion.

When I know for sure
is when Mrs. Strange Sensation
shakes away Hesitation.
I'll step upon the top of the rail
and balance myself.

I'll spread my wings of misery.
I'll slowly lean forward
until I glide with my weight

DOWN
DOWN
DOWN.

The force of the Wind against my face
would choke me,
if I had left Wind.

Wind would force water to my eyes,
if there had been a Wind.

I would feel the warmth of the sun,
if I had left just one.

A bird may have waved at me
as I went downwardly by,
if I had left a sky,
and let them fly.

But I'll go alone.

And only me

will hear me sigh

WHEN
I
DIE.

Oh deep unending darkness
you may roam and you may stray
but just as my heart does burn
at the crossroads where I yearn
you come then turn then lay.

Oh Midnight's death collector
you must rest and you must stay
but just as life has left her
and thus refused its nectar
you are deep sleep's selector
and you chase my dreams away.

I long to dream of those whom I feel
are wonder and beauty
and goodness and real.
I long to roam while my Spirit lies still.
I long to wander on over that hill.

Oh Night you are descending.
Unlike other times you've come
around me your wants are bending
and contending that I am the one.

Oh Sleep my Dreams you're spending
and sending deep thru the sky.
Again I embrace Darkness unending.
And again I will lay down and die.

WINDOW PAIN

BOOK II

1984

I stood
trying to
gaze thru
mirrored windows.

Reflected Back?

My Greatest Sin.

For times too long
I had
been looking out.

Too little time
spent
peering in.

It was midnight
when I began to hear the tapping.
Soft, mysterious rapping sharply tapping
against my window.
The rain was falling.
At first I thought that was the calling
that was tap tap tapping
on my window.

Compelled to rise,
I crossed the room
to end up peering intently outside
across the driveway
past the barn into the meadow.
Seeing
nothing in the darkness
feeling
shivers running thru my body
icy fingers burning up and down my spine.

First I heard thunder. I felt the rumble.
Then illuminating lightning flashed.
I saw her standing there
and she was softly
tap tap tapping at my window.

She was so lovely.
My wildest dream come true was beckoning me
singing
ethereally begging me
to come outside into the storm.
Commanding me to come outside and play.

Although the rain was pouring down
it never touched her
falling all around her
and in the puddles
I saw reflections of her eyes
and I kept the sighs
from welling up inside me.
But I could not move,
standing paralyzed
and transfixed
trying not to stay yet thinking
I would die
if I
could not find the strength
to turn and somehow
walk away.

I only saw her
in those brief moments
when jagged lightning
roared across the darkened skies.
But the vision of her haunting beauty
would not leave me this midnight.
I shut out the sounds
and still heard her soft singing.
Had I not looked
I would not have been able
to remove the sight of her
from my wondering
eyes.

Silk as red as fire
was clinging to her body.
Her hair dark brown
was gently past her shoulders.
There was gold on every finger.
Diamonds sparkled in her ears
and strings of pearls caressed a neck
that seemed as delicate
as a nightly blooming Violet
flower.
Her skin was smooth
perfect
unblemished and her color black
like the unlit skies,
in this midnight hour.

But the power of her beauty
emanated from her soul.
I could see deep in her soul thru my window
into her being.
Bottomless
pools of brown were drowning me.
I was hypnotized and she was pulling me
drawing me
to her within her
I was sinking.
I was helpless to remove her gaze
staring into a maze
into the deepest region of her soul
downwardly spinning into
her beautiful sensuous
dark brown eyes.

Every step she took toward me
I inched forward.
Together
closer
together
we came.
She laid her hands then pressed her face
close against the window pane.
Although I knew danger
I turned my fear to anger.
She was drawing me
near
her voice clear in my mind
her breath blowing in my ear
she was singing
for me only
moaning
for my body
crying for my soul
finally
whispering so wonderfully to me
my own name.

So hot was she speaking
moist steam clouded the window pane.
Closer
ever so closer
to her I came.
With both hands
I touched the glass.

Electric heat crashed thru me!

I tried to shout instead I gasped
my breath escaped me.

Each time I thrashed,
whips of fire lashed thru me.

I asked death to take me.

Like dry ice the window seared me.
I was frozen.
I realized I had mistakenly
chosen.
My sins had not gone unnoticed.
To be scarred was my payment.
Never again
would I appear the same.

If I would disrespect my knowledge
the fact that I knew
only
lonely lost pain
comes tapping at midnight
rapping confidently
aware of my name.

And if I could not reject voices of darkness
standing untouched in pouring rain
I must accept
being a prisoner.
Slave to the mastery
of a burning window pane.

Release me dream I pleaded
it was your love that I needed.
Those sins that are mine
when I made them
I was blinded by fever
in my mind
driven insane
all that time spent searching for you.

A life without love changed me inside.
I took false steps spoke deceiving lies
and tried
to disregard the good
I was put here on Earth to do.
All because I did not have you.
I could not touch you.
My dreams long unfulfilled
began to seem so unreal
I swallowed bitter pills
washed down
by tears I spilled.

My days at home spent thinking
talking to myself about you.
I yearned so hard for you.

My nights alone spent drinking
walking
wandering the Earth for you,
the corners I've turned for you.

On bended knees down on the floor humbled
I asked for you.
What more could I do?
Giving up was left.
Disbelief was all I knew.
Relief I felt
when I released the thought
that kept me pushing on.
Waking up one day I realized
the dream that I'd visualized
was not coming true.

Then in the rain you called my name
bringing me this icy pain.
I could be glad to live my life
just like this.
I would not be sad if death
was just like this
if only close to me
you could remain.

I think I know exactly how you got here.
I don't know precisely why you came.
But I cannot bear up another second
I don't think I can stand up another moment
please tell me.

Who are you?
Please
what is your name?

When she responded
her voice
sounded like an Angel's
pure
clean
how innocently it rang.

Like a bell of conscience
ringing louder than the thunder
her voice
was singing out
pealing vibrations
all thru that
fragile window pane.

Almost a chant
or a sorrowful lament
she squeezed shut her eyes
and I was so wrapped up
so intent in listening
I was caught by surprise.
Tears
tinged red
poured from her eyes
moist lips trembled and I realized
more than a memory
the words were really real
somewhere inside
she could indeed feel.

Lovely woman so strange
red tears
now falling like rain
yet
her expression never changed
soaking wet
her dress
was still unstained
against her breast I saw it cling.
I shut my eyes shook my head no
to what I'd just seen.
I forced myself to believe
what was gradually becoming
apparent.
A dress of fire red silk was turning
transparent.

I could see her wracked with sobs
her chest heaving.
Feel her breath
burning
as if fire she was breathing.
Her heart
I could hear her heart pounding wildly
it was throbbing.
I was terrified.
I knew it was racing much much too fast.

Red tears turning my dream
into a statue of glass.

All this I was watching
a prisoner in my own window.
The pain I was touching I knew
was justified for the many wrongs
I had orchestrated in the past.

Slowly
I was crying.
My tears came from realizing.
Love had burned me thru this window
so I could learn that
just as dreams go
I had faded.
I had lost faith, my soul was jaded
and out of place.
I should have slept and dreamed new dreams
instead of giving up
on the race.

Just as dreams go.
Love will not last unless it exists
in faces and hands of mirrors
subsists in the light of reflection
and resists the treacherous illusion
of a midnight window glass.

Her name?
Temptress she was singing.
Temptress kept on ringing.
And as her tears kept on falling
I found myself calling out to her
asking her to look at me.

She said her mother was Sensation.
She was the daughter of
Temptation
conceived in violation when her mother
had been taken against her will
violently.
Born in pouring rain
left alone with but a name
she was branded by her lips
of passionate fire
her bed a pyre of smoldering emotions
self immolation
corruption and finally destruction
her game.

She could not let me be
she belonged to me.
I had set her free.
Then she turned on me
when I had followed Temptation
accepted false Sensations
giving up my dreams of Love
and decency.

Red tears like rain
expression never changed.
I began to yell her name begging her
to look at me.
Then I screamed her name
and when the fire came
the shattering window pane
threw shards into my heart
slivers into my eyes
blinding me.

My tears turned red and then she said,
although you're blind one day you'll find
more than a dream
Love can be seen
when faces and hands of mirrors
reflect true reality.

When your sight returns again
you must search to see.
If I am false or phantasy.
Reject the lies and realize,
every second every moment
some time will pass.
When dreams are real,
dreams will stand still
existing deep in images
of the mirrored past.

But just as dreams go
there's one thing you must know.

Elusive Love, Reclusive Love
moves on so very fast.

You must start rapping
gently
tap tap tapping.
When you find your loving window
you will know it.

It will have no pain.

No window glass.

REDEMPTIVE JOURNEYS

BOOK III

1984 — 1985

From beneath the brilliant stars
I arose
from my bed in the burning desert sand
to cross snow capped mountains
on my hands
and knees
descend into the valley
to wash away my sins
in the waves
of the deep deep seas.
Hundreds of years ago
on the morning of the second
at exactly three ten
was to begin
within my one moment of eternities
a constant search for salvation.
I shall strive to be relentless
until I arrive
at the end
of my endless
Redemptive Journeys.

VINCENT WARE

TABLE OF CONTENTS

I left riding
not knowing
whether or not I was running
or whether or not I was hiding
from a Love I could never find.

Early morning.
Sun rising. Wind blowing.
I was realizing all these things
at six-forty nine.
Loneliness in my life.
Pain in my heart.
And Love lost
somewhere in my mind.

Riding.
Looking out.
I saw eyes staring!
Staring at me!
Remorsefully?   Hauntingly.
Eyes there!
There in that window glass.

Riding.
Looking back.
My face
pressed against the cold window.
I saw the flowers go.
I saw the buildings go
fading,
fading into a memory
vanishing into the past.

Riding.
Looking up.
I saw dark skies.
Surprised!
Those deathly eyes
looking at me, worrying me.
I saw tears there!
There in that glass
as miles rolled past
I looked at brooding
staring eyes.

Riding.
Looking ahead.
I saw the rain
and when it came
it hid the road,
washed out the sun
and blocked the signs.

Riding in rain.
Repeating her name.
I saw those same
lonely staring eyes.

From deep inside
I realized.
Through all that time
I knew that look
I felt those tears.
I knew those crying eyes
were mine.

The morning sky was grey
dirt grey
and so forboding.
Falling raindrops screaming
cold raindrops scolding.
The earth unspeaking
her voices holding
and I was leaving
many miles unfolding.

That first night black
blind black
the stars were hiding.
I pushed on running
I rolled on riding.
My whole world lost
my purpose sliding.

And I was leaving, I kept on driving.

Where was I going?
What was I trying?
To ease the pain
and cease the lying.
To drown my sins
in goodness crying.

To see again the RED SUN RISING.

Just one more chance
to right my wrongs.
A peaceful sleep
the bed my own.
Please
one more turn
to sing my song.
The words?
My wife, my kids
our home.

Wish one more dream.
That first star shining.
A revelation, this realizing.
I grow older, closer to dying,
can't run too long
can keep on riding
can't give up hope
I'll keep on trying.

Just let the Moon
keep on fading.

Another day
a brand new dawning.

I need to see
the RED SUN RISING.

Sometimes, alone,
I close my eyes and visualize.
I try to see if I can find
somewhere within my mind
THAT LAST TIME.

It's been so very long ago.
In looking back, I couldn't know.

I was so young. She was so young.
Love was beautiful. Love was fun.

We would hold each other
ever so tightly.
We would kiss one another
ever so lightly.
The heats of our bodies
ever so slightly
would cause us to swoon.

Every moment we were together
there existed no Always
no Forever.
Only the thought at first
soft like a feather,
this may be
THAT LAST TIME.

Oh how I loved her
and how she loved me.
There was no doubt
not one uncertainty.

Yet mysteriously we knew
by reading life's signs
although I was her's
and I knew she was mine
this passionate joining
lasting from midnight to morning
still caused fears to begin forming
within us we began learning,
this could very well be,
THAT LAST TIME.

Now I'm lying here scared
and so very lonely.
Years have passed
yet I've loved her only.
She was taken from me
through no wrong of our own.
And from this pain
I know I have grown.
Please believe me and see
all love does not run long.
Every second that will quickly pass
pushes our love further in the past.
This long ago romance could have been
that one chance to make an hour
more than a measure of time.
Our Love was wonderful
and precious and fine.
That Love was the first
in a very long line.
And that may be the last.
Yes, maybe

THAT LAST TIME.

Lying on the too soft bed.
Staring at drab walls
ceilings,
windows full of buildings
dirty,
broken,
empty light fixtures.

It's too hot!
My insides burning.
I'm tossing and turning.
Resolved yet yearning.
I pondered the ingredients
of Love's strange mixtures.

Through far away dreams
poured from turbulent streams
into oceans of steam
I rode the ringing waves
of telephones.
I searched blindly
for the sights
of your pictures.

Wondering why my life
has taken the paths
of separation.
Why I rejoice in the celebration
of touching cold telephones
and caressing old pictures.

Two thousand miles from you,
nobody to know,
nothing to do.
Pacing from wall to wall
past the bedroom hall.
From the door to the mirror
I've worn a lonely line.
Walking and thinking
anticipation sinking.
I'm playing games of imagination
in the chambers of my mind.

Peering into the reflection
of the dark, dusty mirror.
Are those bells or voices?
Do I hear her?

I see lights, images and wispy visions.
The Love I feel
lost in the wishing.
Desire's pain
comes from the missing.
Unfulfilled
my life consisting
of never ringing telephones
never seen pictures.

She said.
When you are gone I lie awake alone.
I think about you.
That I'm without you I know is wrong
and so I cry myself to sleep.

She said, with darkened lights
beneath the covers late at night
she would touch herself
softly, gently, lovingly,
and phantasize with hot desire
as her heat turned into fire
phantasize
that I was strong there
and beside her
then I was long and deep inside her
no matter how she tried
she could not lose this lustful rider.

Then came at last a silent scream
how loveless this love seemed
frustrated tears a restless dream
when reality turned over with the daylight.

How real she learned to phantasize.
Still she yearned to make me realize
that
a love that has no home
is a love that loves alone
this love may waive begin to roam
in a search for an end
to a never ending Phantasy.

She said to me.
I've never known before such kisses.
There is nowhere on my body
or in my soul
you could not reach
you have not touched.

I've never been shown before this passion.
You caress me. You possess me.
My head is spinning
everything at once becomes too much,
too much.

So that is what I want.
That is what I need
when you have gone and I'm alone
beside the phone
waiting for your voice
three thousand miles from me.

I'll always wait for you.

I know now I must make do
with the closeness of a vision
only you and I can see.

If I close my eyes
and Phantasize
we'll come together
in a never ending
Phantasy.

So suddenly
I had woke up.
Looked around then quickly sat up.
The clock,
the hands were pointing straight up.
Confused at first
I could not tell if it was noon
or was it really midnight.

My pillow was wet.
From tears or sweat?
I did not know
and so I rose
now full of things I could not feel
I did not like.

I paced the floor
then opened the door.
Leaning there
I saw the darkness turn
so slowly into daylight.

Then thru the trees
a soft warm breeze
was rustling the leaves
and I heard whispers I heard voices.
Could I believe? I wanted to know
everything, everything,
EVERYTHING,
is gonna be alright, gonna be alright,
it's gonna be alright.

Regrettably
we had broke up.
We should have talked
we could have spoke up.
Hand in hand
we should have walked
we could have made up.
She's left me memories
of lazy mornings
cool moist evenings
hot passionate nights.

I closed the door
then turned around
heaved a sigh sat heavily down.
My head in hands I felt her sounds.
She may be gone
but she could never ever
really leave my sight.
If she comes home
I won't be alone.
If she comes home
everything, everything,
EVERYTHING
is gonna be alright,
gonna be alright,
it's gonna be alright.

There was a noise
and so I sat up.
It was the door and so I stood up.
She walked in
and then she looked up
into my eyes
full of questions full of fright.
She turned around set her bags down.
I saw a smile
so very fleeting, so very slight.

She said,
I know some things are wrong.
I can't stay gone too long.
Your love is much too good
it's much too good
and much too strong.
I missed your smiling in the morning
your hugging in the evening
and your tenderness
especially so, late at night.
Remove this doubt
we'll work things out
then everything
everything,
EVERYTHING,
is gonna be alright
gonna be alright
it's gonna be alright.

Take my hand and come with me
we'll go away and not be found.

We'll leave the world behind us.
I know where we can hide.

And there alone together,
I'll hold you close.
Caress you softly.
Kiss you all over.

You'll begin to feel the fires deep inside.

Your body melting to mine.
Our hearts racing wildly
deep in our eyes this we will surely find.

Flames must have beginnings,
heat needs not have an ending.
There is no level,
there's no limit
to how high your temperature can rise.

Sparks are in the yearnings.
Desires the same as burnings.
The start of fires you'll be learning
begin deep
somewhere
deep inside.

We were lying there
between sometime and somewhere
devoid of concerns, no worries or needs.
Wrapped and protected
in a picnic blanket
we were feeling serene
and secure and pleased.
The fragrance of flowers
eased through the air
the heats of desire
wafted on the breeze.

Laughing and running
from a brief summer shower
we discovered we had wound up under
a very old
and mysteriously beautiful
hanging
Weeping Willow Tree.

Pulsing sounds
we could hear as we kissed
moaning noises
begging us please.
Moist ethereal voices
somehow from deep in that tree
were whispering
sighing softly
come with me,
come with me,
come with me.

It was hot
that early August summer evening.

Ominous clouds at first hovering near
dissipated becoming less threatening
a cooling wind was blowing gently
so slowly the sky had cleared.
The last of the sunset
had just disappeared.
The first of the stars had again reappeared.

Suddenly something was stirring
a force seemed extremely powerful.
Aroused with interest
we were calm and curious
full of wonder, empty of fear.

It was LUST!
Languidly moving
it had turned and then it had reared.
First, a scream of agony,
second this anguished cry.
Touch me for I am growing,
feel my teeming pride!
I am spawned
from the beginnings of yearning.
I am nourished on flesh that is burning.
I garner my pleasure
when I know you are learning
that I was born am indeed alive.

I am LUST!
An unconscionable animal
excessive demands,
my hunger, unreasonable
unrepressive, it's very conceivable,
never will I be satisfied.

Cast off the bonds of consciousness!
Surrender yourself and you will arrive.
I will impart to you my roads of ecstasy
but I am the chauffeur
you must let me drive.
I know of paths you have never seen before
lacking my direction they are never tried.
Then when we reach my destination
looking back you will recognize
you were traveling up and down
in and out, all around
on a runaway roller coaster ride.

Lightning flashed and thunder rumbled
a torrent of rain streamed from the sky.
Steam began forming all around us
fires raging everywhere inside.
We could not control the motion
hold back the waves
or stem the tides.
We were swimming and drowning
as if in the ocean
slipping and sliding
down a glass mountain.

Hypnotized we were looking.
Oh! What was this feeling?
From where burns this fire?
What did we know? How fast could we go?
Were we just dreaming?
What were we screaming?
What did we see? What did we see?
What did we see that warm summer evening
lying beneath
that Willow Tree?

We saw at the same time
we were walking that same line
we were feeling the same thing
simultaneously.
We denied we could kill it
and we cried we could feel it.
From deep within
the power pulled us
next, strenuously began to shove.
The earth was reeling and whirling below us
that Tree was urging us on from above.
Whispering:
You are alone there exists no others.
In you joining
you are much more than Lovers.
This evening has meaning,
because you're in Love.

It was there in our eyes.
At the very same time we both realized.

We were coming together!
It was lasting forever!
I was coming with her
and she was coming with me
coming with me
coming with me.

We'll never forget that evening
or those feelings.
Such intensity!
She said she felt the flames
rushing out of her.
I could feel the fire pouring out of me.

Waking to the warmth
of an early August summer morning.

Huddled against the chill
of a cold December.

In our minds we will always remember.
In our eyes we will always see.

Look through those raindrops falling
there lies the truth, what we believe.

Rain that falls is not rain at all
just rapturous tears flowing
from that WEEPING WILLOW TREE.

Let's talk about this thing called Love
for just a moment.

It's something I've not so far
been able to keep for very long.
It gets quite hard to understand
something you only recognize off and on.

I wonder,
where is It when you don't have It
or feel It?
Where does It go? Where does It hide?
Does It exist somewhere out there
or when It's not around
does It always remain buried inside?
It's such a strange and unusual feeling.
I think everyone finds It difficult,
if not impossible to describe.
It appears to be such an important thing.
It's talked about all the time.
It seems to be everywhere all at once.
Then all of a sudden It's hard to find.
Some people can get It and hold on forever.
Some people only touch It in their minds.

How can It be so many things,
so many different things?
It can be so strong. It can be so weak.
It can be both good and bad.

Love can heal.
But there is no pain like the pain of Love.
Have you ever had Love squeeze your heart?
It's a wonderful feeling
until It loses control
and tears it apart.

Cry! Cry sad tears.
Cry! Cry happy tears.
Cry until you can't cry any longer.
Suffer and die,
until you can't die any longer.
Go without and you will starve
until you hunger again
and again and again.

We should talk about It.

In spite of this all,
there is no other power,
no other feeling
like the Current Of Love.

The Current runs from one to the other,
then back again.
To truly love someone is wonderful.
To have someone love you back, at the same time
is the greatest experience of all.
When I talk about Love,
that's what I'm talking about.

Because
when I wrap my arms around Her, My Love,
I want Love to hug me back.
And when I kiss Her and caress Her all over,
in return, I also want that.
I want to breathe
the pungent fragrance of desire
and drink the burning juices of fire
when I taste My Love.
Time we must not waste My Love.
In the never ending race of love
we don't know how far
The Current Of Love will run
we do know It moves so very fast.
We don't know anything
of the future of love
or where It's gone
when It's disappeared in the past.
It seems to have a beginning a middle
and certainly an end.

But when I love Her and she's my Love
if she loves me
I'll be Her Love, no matter the years,
the days, the hours,
or the moments that must inevitably pass.
It takes two to truly consist of love.
The Current Of Love
will only exist thru love.
Since we cannot really resist this love,
together let's make our Current Of Love
last, and last, and last.

I want to cry
but I know I can't.

I'm a man
a man can't cry.
I'd rather die. I'd rather die.
I cannot let my woman see me cry.

I'll take the knife, I'll take the gun
commit that crime refuse to run
again a man has just become
another senseless suicide.

I want to cry
but I know I can't.

I must hide this pain inside.
I can't show fear, I can't shed tears.
I bolt the door I'm now at home
and if I cry, I cry alone.
Don't see me cry, I'd rather die.
I can't cry if I'm a man.
Please hold me close and take my hand.
Say these words:
You're still my man go on and cry.
I understand you're still my man.
I understand, I understand.

I want to cry
but I know I can't.

I'd rather lie, I'd rather die.
I'll take the knife I'll take the gun
commit that crime refuse to run
again a man has just become
another senseless suicide.

The world won't let a man be all he can.
Women can't seem to understand.
Distracted views can't realize
sometimes a man would rather die
than let his woman see
deep in his eyes
that he can feel that he is real
a man can kill a man can die
never, ever
should a man be seen to cry.

Please hold me close.
Please take my hand.
Say the words you understand.
A man can cry still be a man.
I'll be a man, I'll be your man.

Sometimes the world becomes so cold.
Sometimes the pain can't be controlled.
I feel tired, I feel old.
I take the key and lock the door.
Shut in at home I'm on my own
and if I cry, I cry alone.
Must cry alone.

I've been Distorted!
I've gazed upon dark stars
in the early morning light.
I've felt the burning of the sun
in the middle of the night.
I've spun around looked up at down
and wondered what is left
when love's no longer right.
You see,
I've been Distorted.

Mist within my eyes
when I knew I could not cry.
My breath upon the wind
even though I could not sigh.
My heart amongst the clouds
I've known my soul could fly.

And Love's been just a dream
that never seems to die.

Chaos!
Self destruction and confusion.
Your name imagined with illusion.
This delusion
was pre-ordered.
My life is cluttered
and un-sorted.
This the end it's been recorded.

I've been Distorted.

When I was a boy
I couldn't see
beyond tomorrow
the furthest reaching
of my sorrow
was whether or not
I could go out to play.
I didn't know.

When I was young
I couldn't see beyond
the street
on down, the sidewalk
only reached
the corner candy shop
I was small
and I walked slow.

A little while later
I crossed
the red light
to the drug store
to a new world
full of new things
full of new sights
and new people
I didn't know.

I didn't know about
stores torn down
phantasies made, memories lost
and painful sounds.

I woke at fifteen
not looking at sixteen.
My young eyes it was not seen
that I would drive
all by myself out on my own.
I now had grown and I had gone
to a basement dance
on the other side
of town.

And so I learned
of holding hands
of beautiful smiles
and lovely eyes
soft moist lips
and warm strong thighs
dancing close
around and around and around.
That first love felt.
That first time touched.
That first love found.

I flew past eighteen.
My first job. My own place.
There in the mirror
a different face?
A little more work.
A lot less play.
I fell, I crawled,
I walked, I ran.
Perhaps it's so? Yes I can!
Twenty one.
I'm now a man.

At twenty five
another start
begin again.
Third real love.
Second pain.
Fourth true end.
Aging name.
Same
young heart.

I didn't know.

I didn't know
how pain was sold.
Why lies are told.
How love burns cold.
That's why men turn bold.
I didn't know.

At thirty five
a brand new car
a second home
all that I have
I own alone.

I didn't know
that being real
and loving true
was not the way
or thing to do.
Strange thoughts
I still had not
out grown.

Kindness and caring
is wrong.
Harshness and fear
remains strong.
No one that is good
stands long.
Youth must remain in the past.
Nothing goes on and on.

Stores torn down.
First loves lost.
Loves unfound.
Fires turn cold.
I grow old.
And long ago
to me
these words were told.

Honey,
one day you must learn how to play.
You can't keep giving all your things away.
Now you're sitting here
and there goes your little girlfriend
on your new bicycle riding past.
You just can't be nice all the time
they say nice people end up last.

I didn't know.

You know,
to tell the truth, which you already know.
I'm both humbled and scared
to be standing before you like this.
I can't hide from you the fact that
until now I could not accept you could exist.
My life was such a puzzle
sometimes the pieces did not fit.
You can tell by the way I'm standing
I'm much too weak to try to sit.
The time has come
to accept the wrong I've done
and what I'm getting ready to say to you
we all sometimes at last admit.
Forgive me please. Forgive my sins.
Forgive the things I've done
to cause you sorrow.
I could not comprehend
I could not understand
that one day I would be before you begging,
pleading for just one more tomorrow.
I know there are things,
good things, I should have done.
With another time around
I won't walk and I won't run.
I'll stand there,
evil swirling all around me
I won't gaze upon my old friends,
I won't turn, I will not follow.

Please give me one more chance.
Please give me one more breath.
Please just give me one more tomorrow.

I was sitting on a bench at a bus stop.
My eyes looked down my head was bent.
Oblivious at noon, early days of June,
I could not feel the warmth
of the hot summer sun.
I shivered from worry
acknowledged the twilight
I knew what the darkness brought
for thirty days
I had known what time passing lent.

How absurd or was it ironic
on this day my birthday
I would be cast away,
away from my dank, dark,
rat and roach infested room
a room that was my home.
I lived all alone
down the second landing
past the storage bins
deep, banished deep in a tenement basement.
One thing had followed another
a stream of nightmarish events.
I held receipts for my misdeeds
delinquent notes were now past due.
Repeated sins turned out indecent.
I was being paid well
for my transgressions.
But just as broken lies
will not come true
mistreated lives can't cash for new
and old bad checks won't pay the rent.

Evil hearts returned to maker
marked, feelings insufficient
punishment only
accepted as payment.

Hard luck had dogged me now
for two and a half long years.
The pressure would not ease
there was no such thing as soft relent.

My soul had come up bankrupt.
My time wasted, my life spent.
I had lost my youthful dream
of a golden road
I didn't know where it was
or where it went.

And so the twists and turns I'd taken
had brought me to the last stop
whispering, saying words of forgiveness
at the bus stop
shivering, praying words in twilight,
I thought I knew
what the darkness meant.

And then,
reflecting from beneath a leaf
was just a corner.
Lying in the gutter, nicked,
scraped, still shiny, slightly bent
a coin, a quarter.
I had found myself twenty five cents.

I placed the coin into my hand
but I could not understand
the burning that ran
all the way through me.
Knocked onto my knees,
begging, crying please
it would not let me be
I could not shake that quarter free.
The pain was so intense
I passed out beside that bench
and I dreamed I heard voices
singing softly
over and over again the words repent.
You must repent.

I awoke to a stillness
and a death like darkness
the only light, I was holding in my hand.
Glowing was a brand, a vivid imprint
of a coin of twenty five cents.
The words In God We Trust were there!
Lit up in the blackness!
From deep in my soul
I knew exactly what they meant.
God had come to me in His Glory.
Through His power there would be no sorrow
to the end of my story.
His Goodness was within me
and through me
this message would always be sent.
I would tell the world
I found God in a quarter in the gutter.
I found God in twenty five cents.

I'm getting ready to leave now.
I've got my things together
and when I walk on out that door
you won't see me any more.
I'm gonna leave now.

I'm tired I want to go.
I was confused but now I know.

There's no end to this in sight.
I can't tell what's wrong
what's right.
I finally understand
this tunnel that I'm in
has no end

has no light

so I'm leaving now.

Goodbye.

RESOLUTIONS

BOOK IV

1987 — 1988

Behold me NOW!
Once propelled on a flight of fear
through the White Rains of the lonely sky
in shivers
I have finally landed.
Not to die
but to be reborn.
I had turned
from the mirrored Windows of Pain
struck out
across the burning desert in my mind
only to find myself
on my knees encircled in flames
my Journey of Redemption vanishing in smoke.
Yet I have risen
from the ashes I stand naked
protected by the reality of Truth
and the strength of Love.
I have laid down the sword of anger.
Stepped from behind
my invisible inferior shield
and stripped insufficiency, inadequacy,
and anxiety from my body.
Liquid repression poured into the ocean.
Powdered evasion blown into the wind.
I rejoice in the Triumph
of my deepest longing desire.
All I ever truly sought was joy and peace
and freedom from the excruciating
FIRE.

TABLE OF CONTENTS

As a child.
Standing at the back screen door
bouncing, humming,
softly singing, joyously watching
the first little orange breasted Robin
come ushering
Spring in.
Yet,
all the while behind your fearful smile
deep down you were really trying
to ignore the sounds of Momma
on the bedroom floor
crying.

Daddy gone, but coming home to you.
You really knew,
on the phone the promising voice
he wasn't really trying.

As a child.
The Sun of Summer
replaced the warming hugs you could not know
but sensed you missed.
How many times were you held, and
listened to and rocked in loving arms
to sleep?
How often were you kissed?
Rewards forever to keep.

As a child.
Remember Autumn?

The beautiful leaves had fallen.
And as you watched there standing
in the smoldering smoke
after their burning
visions within the ashes
mesmerizing, hypnotizing
vague notions darkly rising.
Yearning, to run out on your own
around the block, down the alley
over the fence,
across the yard up the back porch
and through your window.
Hide, under the bed alone.
What is that feeling, deep inside
churning?
What do you fear
when you near her voice
calling you home?

As a child.
In Winter,
sucking icicles, building snowmen.
Finally, banging on the side door
to be let in, into her arms, into her heart.
Into the very words that she was whispering.
At last confessing it all.
She took you through Spring on into the Fall.
The message was sent her
that evening in Winter.
Too soon, too young and yet you were told
how hands once soft turned rough and cold
why eyes turned cloudy
and beautiful youth too quickly grew old.

Momma,
be there as a mirror for your Baby.
Let your smiling eyes reflect the joy you find
in the wonderous miracle
of the presence of your laughing Baby.
Be there with your touch.
The Baby needs to sense so much
that gentleness and safety lives there
in your protective embrace.
Momma, love that Baby when that Baby cries.

Daddy,
be there as a ladder of stone for your Child.
Let the strength within your arms
guide that stumbling Child.
Lift up that fallen Child
over those broken steps.
Be a mirror of confidence, integrity
and bearer of truth.
Let that Child learn that
behind the gruff deepness of your voice
there is respectful love
and there need not be fear of you.
Daddy,
love that Child when that Child cries.

Momma, if you did not have love to give
to your Baby and
Daddy, if you could not share your self
or care for the Child you helped make
and you walk, away too soon
then,

Someone
be there for those out there
who are lost and alone,
invisible in a crowded world.
Reaching out for a touch
that was never felt.
Listening for words never spoken.
Missing strength and praise never given.
Searching for love that was never known.
Locked down and frozen in emotional time.
Unable to let the Baby within know.
Unable to help the Child within grow.
Unable to let the pain within go.

Turning away and hiding.
Running away and waiting
to be saved.

Waiting,
and waiting,

for Someone.

Woman.
I have loved you, desired you, for so long.
I can not remember from where or when
but there was always ambivalence there.
Drawn to You.
Chasing You.
Running from You.
Catching You.
Losing You.
I used to be afraid of You.
I used to be afraid of what You might say.
I used to be afraid of what You might do
if you knew
I was afraid of You.

Words
had welled up inside me
until they fell upon paper
like tears
trying to sort out and understand the fears.

What to do? Afraid of You.

Woman.
Lovely. So beautiful.
So mysteriously strange.
So fresh.
Always so frighteningly wonderfully new.
Reaching out hesitently to me
and I tentatively extending myself to You.
Oh how I used to be afraid of You.

The pain had come and so I ran away.
Off I flew, deep into my thoughts
to find You in fanciful places
imaginary memory traces. Dreams
reflecting warm receptive smiling faces.
And in these dreams it seems You knew
how I wanted, You.
To touch and love, You.
You read my mind and yes, You knew
all those things I wanted to do.

But dreams are dreams
and are not true.
Dreams are borderline illusions
and very soon, mine became delusions.
Driven was I to the reality of You.
Then directly, for the first time I looked
at You,
wondering if indeed you truly knew.
I was lonely woman, and afraid of You.

At that moment I realized
behind your concealing seductive eyes
reside the answers the reasons why
You act the way You do.
I recognized the hurt
the images of angry disappointment,
the loneliness I knew.
All that time I was afraid
of You,

You were afraid
of me too.

Wish that you were with me now
as I awaken
from this blinding sleep.
Wish that you were here beside me now
to discover
all that I see as I find it.
Wish that you were giving me now
what you possess,
that missing part of me.
Wish that you were hearing me now
speaking of you.
Wish that you were tasting my kiss
and feeling my touch.
Long have I missed you, so strong, so much.
I'm aching for you.
I'm reaching for you.
Soon, will very soon
become now.
Then we will be together.

Something in your smile
so powerfully alluring.
Beauty in your smile.
Much more than a look
mysteriously
a message.
In your lovely eyes.
Urges in your voice
whispering, enticing.
Such sensuous words.
Hearing your moist sounds
tempting
enthralling.
Unbelievable sounds.
Then sensing your breath
very wickedly
blowing so closely.
I was losing my mind.
Then feeling your touch
rousing, inciting.
So amazing that touch.
Next tasting your lips
scorching, searing.
Fire burning that kiss.
Giving over to me
truly tenderly
so wonderfully
meant only for me.

I surrendered my Love.

Across the tranquility of my mind there stood in isolation that landscaped moment that appears clear and exact. A suspended monument to the instant it's all over.

Moans and sighs between the lustful utterances once exhorting me on in quiet screams and demanding whispers begin then to subside. Slowly they fade to a murmur. The cries have quieted. Is it all over?

Feeling the rushing hearts begin to ease, I caress you lightly, and my shocking touch passes across the sticky moisture just a while ago aflame, now drying and cooling beneath my fingers.

I still taste you on my lips. Delicious, delicate, sensitive you. I know you through your timeless mind and behind the darkness of my half shuttered eyes I see you with every breath as I breathe the air hanging heavy with your pungent fragrance and I ponder on what else remains when we're done and it's gone and over.

I loathe to stir, least the substance of this instance be disturbed and seconds lost. Words are needless in this silence of dispersing passion. Any movement or sound may mean it's really over.

As I dreamingly reflect upon you, I reminisce about how I used to be,and I can recall the emptiness these ephemeral occasions once held for me. The transitory fear, this type of fleeting sense of finality.

To offer myself to a stranger was traumatic to me. Rejection was always too natural to see. Then with the end I would turn quickly before they could turn from me. Realizing something was missing, I rose with disappointment urging me, to wash away the dejection. Cleanse away the guilt, the shame, sterilize the pain and towel away the naked memory.

Retrospective remembrances so vague in passing, so heavy, so fast, of meaningless emotionless affairs that never had a chance to last, blown away on the winds of insecurity.

Here in my arms in the outline of your slightly hidden silhouette I touch more than warm, wet softness. I recognize your tenderness and the surrenderings to your vulnerability. Surrounded in this relation of loving reality, we can extend our belief through the wonderful ecstasy. Expend again. Begin again the start of eternity. Real Love can never conclude climacticly.
It shall not end.

True Love can never, ever, be over.

I shall see you always as freshness
in my morning eyes
in the rising of the light.
Not just in a glance and never in an
inattentive trance
but really see you.
And if displeasure should pass you
like a cloud
no matter how brief or very slight
never could this vision hide from me
I would know. I would see
and I shall try to help you smile
always.

I will hear you in the noon.
Not distractedly or impatiently
but surely hear you.
I will hearken to your every spoken word.
And if there is loneliness there
or desire between your sounds,
I would know.
Or if there is anger beneath your words
you need never plead to be heard.
I will try to understand you at all times
in all ways.

I will touch you in the evening
with all my passion and genuine meaning
before anything or anyone else, for you.
I will caress you in all the ways
you have taught me to do.
And when my arms enfold you
if ever you were weary
I would know and I would support you gently.
I would hold you always.

I will taste you in the nightime
I would searchingly look
and knowingly find
the essence of your everlasting beauty
not only in the flavor of your loving body,
I would savor always the wonder and the
mystery within the power of your mind.
The memory of your taste will remain with
me always.

I will want you for ever and ever
across unlimited sunsets
beyond uncountless moons.
And if we were to be separated
I would know the brightest stars
should lead me home to you.
If it took all eternity
I would come back to you.
I need to be with you.
I will want you always.

What do you DESIRE
when you are alone
in the wee moments of the early mourning
when all is dark and silent
and you toss and turn confused
and concerned about the future
of an endless tomorrow, what do you want?
What do you want
when there is just yourself and nobody else?
No one to claim? No one to blame?
No one to lead? No one to follow?
No one to please?
No one to cause pain and sorrow?
Where lie your needs?
Do your whispers turn to the skies,
or do you search for the reasons inside?
What do you believe?
Do you believe in magic, sorcery,
incantations, rituals,
pageantry or voodoo?
Do you hold on to gold and paper
and jewels and use them as totems
to soothe the fears to ward off taboos
that push on you and pressure your mind
as you stand there naked in the darkness,
in the dim reflection
of the demanding mirror, what do you wish?

What do you see, when do you look,
into the truth, reach in your mind,
deep in the corners, what do you find?
Who do you ask?
Can you scream out what you really want?
Do you want wisdom and answers
that will build you a bridge
across the suffocating mire?
What does your life require?
When will you learn,
that as long as you yearn,
for happiness, through the people,
places and things you acquire,
forever will you lack,
forever will you want.
Never will you satisfy DESIRE.

Let me die in Peace with my Self.
Let me die with books beside me,
a pen in my hand
and my face pale and cold upon blank paper.
Let me die wielding an ink stained weapon
poised against the injustice
of those who have come before me
and forced lies into me knowingly,
those unknowingly passing ignorance on
and those in awe of Reality
trying to find solace in illusions
that must inevitably
crumble beneath the power of a being
that thinks and reasons
and trusts in its Self.

Let me die unafraid of my Self.
Let me die
having become a friend for my Self.
Let the echos of my voice
and the outline of my symbols
reflect the tragedy of the waging battles
that pit us against one another
in an endless raging war.

Let me die with acceptance of your Self.
Let me die
with an understanding for our Self.
Let me die with a Love for Self.
Let me die wondering.
Let me die pondering.
Let me die questioning.

Let me die asking Why?!

What may point to Which.
Where will show me there
and When provides the Time.
Only Why
will give the Reason.

Only why
shall tell the purpose.
Only Why
will cause the answers
to free my stagnant soul
and soothe my troubled mind.

Why will let me die
in Serenity with my Self.

Years. Days. Hours.
Moments gone forever
but that's alright Today.
I was lost and confused.
I did not know my way.
But even in the abysmal chasm
I was trying.
Lovers gone, pictures misplaced.
The visages of loveliness begin to fade
never to be seen in clarity again.
Nothing I can do about that.
So, that's alright today.
Another sunrise looms just over the horizon.
I'll keep on trying.
If I linger in the past
reminiscing of last years sorrows
I most surely will miss
the beauty of tomorrow.
Only depressions lie in longing
to alter yesterdays.
I'm not afraid to keep on trying.
Should I have tried harder?
Could I have known better?
Regrets, remorse behind me.
Guilt slowly eases away.
In the back of my memories
will I hear what the voices say?
Still I know they shall sometimes call.
But,
that's alright today.
It's better to have loved and lost
than never to have loved at all.

Sometimes I hear echos faintly,
ever so insistently reverberating
resoundingly summoning me.
And sometimes
I hear soft footsteps that today I realize
have coupled with ghostly whispers
to furtively direct and influence me.
Yes, I hear footsteps
and were I to follow
they would be leading me away,
away from the Love and Serenity
I have uncovered after an arduous journey
and tormenting search
existing since the birth of my time.
I hear these hints
and demanding invitations requesting
I regress back in my thoughts
back to those same old feelings
back to the actions of yesterdays
step outside of reality and slip secretly
over the line.
I hear vague commands enticing me
urging me to come quietly
into the childish darkness
dimly   seep
into the recesses
of the cavernous labyrinth
innocently   creep
into unconscious insanity
sleep
with drowsy banality
weep, deep in the depths of my mind.

Although
once that world held comforting memories
in my desirous delirious imageries
and long ago there appeared to be clarity
in shadows and lonely phantasies
today I know what's awaiting me
I have belief in the pain I would find.

For in that life of repressive solitude
there lurks chaotic disorder
borderless boundaries
synaptic signals
mis-read symbols
and devious confusing signs.

Also,
today I know the cognitive dissonance
was in the look of my eyes only
my glance was truly distorted
and my sight had surely been blind.

Today
I heed not the discording voices
or follow meandering rhymes.
Today I have new variating choices
that shall waste not my last precious times.

I remember the wandering walking
turning a thousand circles
I discovered ten thousand imprints
made in turmoil from circuitous footprints
and each footstep had truly been mine.

There shall be Knowledge!
There shall be Peace!
There shall be Love!
But how
and where are these needs found?

Search the skies
above the clouds far beyond the mountains?
Withing the hues of watery oceans
within the rivers
of ruby red rainbow fountains?
Dig deep to the depths
of the hidden earthly fortress
into the damp darkness
of forbidden ground?

I glanced above.
I probed across.
I traveled down.
Over and over and over again.
Around and around and around.

Never would I Have what I could not be.

I looked at last
inside of me.

Never could I Give what I could not be.
Uncovered the Locks.
Discovered the Key.
Inside my mind.
Inside of me.

The treasure I sought so endlessly
was inside my mind.
Inside of me.
The fear I felt so frighteningly
was of my thoughts, depressing me,
pushing at me unconsciously
inside of me.
So wrong so blind I could not see
alone so long I was lonely for me.
Unhappy with me.
Disappointed with me.
Angry with me. Punishing me.
Disapproving of me.
Disbelieving in me.
Mourning for me. Unconsciously.
Turmoil. Inside of me.

I was running from me.
I was hiding from me.

And then I find through all that time,
I owned the answers I had the key.

Opening my eyes enlightening to see.
The Love I want first comes For me.
I must Love me.

I must be healthy. I shall be joyful.
I shall know peace. I will be free
Inside my Heart. Inside my Soul.
From my Mind.

Inside of Me.

Such wonder in This World!

As I stand here on the other side
I look back at yesterdays,
across the course my passage has forged.

I can see for many years
and countless miles.

What a fascinating quest it's been,
and yet, what a dangerous journey it was.
And I am proud
to be standing here on the other side
of pain
on the other side of loneliness
on the other side of fear
on the other side of hatred
on the other side of chaos
here I stand enlightened,
on the other side of Darkness.

What a generous and marvelous thing
This Life,
to accept all my external trapings
and my worldly possessions
as payment for my crossing.
And in exchange
I received the most glorious gift,
a change of mind about my Self.

And as I turn toward tomorrows,
toward the light,
I have all I'll ever need
for the charges of the future,
an understanding of my essence.
No greater wealth exists
than an honest, revealing,
penetrating, accepting insight.
In order to be right I must see right.
And as I begin this exciting new path
I know what lies ahead.
I know what I will eventually have.

I will have friends because now
I can be a friend.
I will have real happiness because today
I can really be happy.
I will know what it is to have peace
because,
I will know what it is like
to be peaceful.
I will have true love because,
I can truly be loving.

All that I have I must give
in order to keep
that which I have gained.

There is new work to be done.

These are the rules here on the other side.

What rewards there are in This Life
here, on the other side!

But I must keep my eyes open and follow
the righteous signs.
I've been instructed
that those arrows that point
to the truth of reality will never fail me.
They will always direct me
to the same place,
time after time after time.
The commandments here insist that
I must maintain
a constant sense of harmony
between the three structures
of my personality
and then I will find that serenity
exists within these regions of my mind.

Such is this world here on the other side
that there will forever be a Lantern
lit up in brilliance thru out the night.
I can see everything in all directions.
Here it's warm and beautiful and bright.
Come join me.
Not there,
in the Darkness of lonely shadows.
I'm over here waiting patiently for you
on the other side.

Follow me,
and step into the splendid light.

I The Cloak,
Encircled My Soul In A Soft, Warming,
Layered Garment
A Coat,
Protection Against The Dampening Rains.
Raised Kerchief,
My Loving Caress Upon My Face, Expunged Away
The Moistened Stains.
I The Candle,
Illuminating, Luminous, Beacon Bright,
Had Crippling Thoughts,
Was Injuriously Lame.
Light Up The Sashless, Transparent Window
Thru Which I Journey, A Quest For Fame.
Onward!
Toward The Glowing, Smoldering Pyre.
Behind! Leave Behind The Painful Pane.
I The Charioteer,
Lashed The Steed Phoenix
Over The Abyss Of Loneliness
Across The Bridge Of Fear
Above The River Shame.
Down The Road Frustration
Into The Roaring Valley I Came.
I The Redeemer,
At One Time Spurned By My Self
Burned By My Own Desire,
Enlightened By A Search For Knowledge
I Discovered My Name.
I As Truth,
Yearned For The Test Of Fire.
Sought I,
The Purifying Flame.